Duke of Albany
(Goneril's husband)

Duke of Cornwall
(Regan's husband)

**Earl of
Gloucester**
(father to Edmund
and Edgar)

Edmund
(Gloucester's illegitimate son)

Edgar / Poor Tom
(Gloucester's son)

Earl of Kent / Caius
(Lear's adviser/servant)

Oswald
(Goneril's servant)

5

King Lear was old and had grown tired of ruling his kingdom, so he decided to give a share of his lands to each of his daughters. But first he wanted to hear how much they loved him.

Goneril, Lear's eldest daughter, who was married to the Duke of Albany, said, "I love you more than I can ever say. You are dearer to me than my life and freedom."

Lear's second daughter, Regan, who was married to the Duke of Cornwall, tried hard to outdo her sister. "I love you far more than Goneril ever could!" she protested.

Finally, Lear turned to his youngest daughter, Cordelia, who was being courted by both the King of France and the Duke of Burgundy.

"How much do *you* love me, Cordelia?" asked the old king.

Cordelia had always been very close to her father but she wanted to be quite honest. She knew that Goneril and Regan were just flattering him. All they really cared about was getting control of the kingdom.

"I love you as much as a daughter should love her father," she replied. "Why do my sisters have husbands if they can love no one but you, Father? If *I* ever marry, I will give my husband at least half my love."

However, King Lear had been fooled by Goneril and Regan. They had told him exactly what he wanted to hear and so he couldn't see how greedy they were. Lear took Cordelia's honesty as an insult, and instantly grew angry.

"You won't inherit a penny," the king snarled at her. "Your share of my kingdom will be divided equally between your sisters!"

He paused, shaking with emotion, then turned to Goneril and Regan. "I shall still be called king. But my sons-in-law, Albany and Cornwall, will govern. I shall keep a hundred knights with me always, and I will live in each of your castles for a month at a time."

Goneril and Regan smiled sweetly, but saw that their father's moods could be troublesome.

"Cordelia was only trying to be honest with you, sir," said the Earl of Kent, the king's most loyal adviser, trying to calm him down.

But the king was blinded by anger. "If I ever see you again, Kent, I'll have you executed!" he roared.

Lear was even more determined to punish Cordelia. He called in the King of France and the Duke of Burgundy, who were both hoping to marry her.

"My daughter Cordelia will now have no dowry," announced Lear. "Do either of you still want to marry her?"

The Duke of Burgundy backed away immediately. But the King of France lovingly took Cordelia's hand. "Come with me to France and reign as my queen," he said to her.

The Earl of Gloucester's illegitimate son,
Edmund, paced the hall of his father's castle,
plotting and planning. He had always been
jealous of his half-brother Edgar, their father's
heir. But now he had a plan to turn his father
against Edgar and get him banished. Then the
way would be clear for Edmund himself to inherit
everything! He had forged a letter signed with
Edgar's name, outlining a plot to kill their father.

When the Earl of Gloucester joined his son, Edmund made sure that he saw him trying to hide the letter in his pocket.

"Give me that at once!" demanded Gloucester.

When he read the letter, Gloucester was shocked.

"Don't worry, Father," said Edmund, delighted his evil plan was working so well. "I'll find out what's going on."

*W*hen Edmund found his brother, he told him, "Father seems angry with you, Edgar."

Edgar was perplexed. "Someone has been telling lies about me," he replied.

"You may be right," said cunning Edmund. "Just stay out of Father's sight until he's calmed down. And perhaps you should arm yourself…"

While Edmund was misleading his father and betraying his brother, King Lear and his hundred knights were spending their first month with Goneril. The banished Earl of Kent, out of love for his king, had secretly returned in disguise as a servant called Caius. "I can still serve the king," he thought, "and perhaps he will pardon me."

The old king's jester also kept him company, but mocked him and played tricks on everyone, including Caius.

Goneril found her father's presence in her house annoying. "I can't possibly put up with all your knights," she told Lear. "They're behaving so badly that my palace is more like a tavern."

Lear was furious at such lack of respect. "I'm not staying here to be insulted," he shouted. "I have another daughter who will make me more welcome. I'll stay with Regan!" Cursing Goneril, he sent Caius ahead with a message for Regan.

Goneril's husband, the good-hearted Duke of Albany, was angry with his wife.

But Goneril had a ready answer. "Can't you see my father's knights are a danger to us? With their help he can do anything he likes. I'll send my steward, Oswald, with a note to Regan warning her not to let him keep so many."

$\mathcal{A}$t his father's castle, Edmund learned that Regan and Cornwall were expected that evening. This could only help his plans. Calling Edgar from his hiding place Edmund told him, "Father's coming. Someone must have given you away. We'll pretend to fight, otherwise he might think we've been plotting together!"

Reluctantly, Edgar agreed. The brothers drew their swords. At the height of the battle, Edmund told Edgar to make his escape. Then Edmund deliberately wounded himself.

When Gloucester appeared, Edmund claimed that Edgar had attacked him.

"But why?" asked Gloucester, troubled.

"Edgar wanted me to kill you, Father. But naturally I refused," Edmund lied.

Gloucester was shocked. "Edgar must be arrested. Edmund, you shall inherit my lands."

The delighted Edmund tried his best to look upset.

Gloucester greeted his guests and told Regan and Cornwall about Edgar's wicked plans to murder him.

"Yes, Edgar is friendly with my father's unruly knights," Regan said. "He's obviously been under their bad influence." Then she turned to Edmund and said, "But we certainly need supporters who are as loyal as you."

Edmund bowed, smirking with pleasure.

*K*ent rode to Gloucester's castle disguised as
Caius, carrying Lear's letter to Regan. On the
way, he met Goneril's sevant, Oswald. He
guessed that he carried letters from Goneril, full
of disrespect for the king. Drawing his sword,
Kent began a fight.

But when Cornwall and Regan heard about it,
Lear's servant was ordered to be put immediately
into the stocks.

Horrified that the king's messenger could be treated like a common thief, Gloucester pleaded for his release. But Regan refused to listen.

*W*hen Lear arrived at Gloucester's castle, he was furious to see his servant in the stocks. "This is a personal insult," he snapped. "I must see my daughter *now!*"

But it was some time before Regan and her husband appeared. Denying that her sister could have treated the king disrespectfully, Regan told Lear to return and beg Goneril's forgiveness.

Then Goneril herself arrived at the castle, smiling her usual sweet smile.

When Lear begged Regan for support, she took Goneril's hand tenderly. "Go back with my sister and try and live peacefully with her," she advised her father. "And dismiss at least fifty of your knights."

Finally, the king lost his temper. "I vow vengeance against you hags!" he swore and staggered furiously out into the night accompanied by his faithful jester.

Although a violent storm was brewing, Regan ordered the gates to be locked, shutting her father out on the deserted moor.

Lear's mind was in such turmoil that he ignored the torrential rain. His thoughts wandered and he ranted loudly about 'ungrateful daughters'.

Eventually, the Earl of Kent found the king. Kent had been released from the stocks, but was still disguised as Caius. "You shouldn't be outside

on a night like this, sir," he said to Lear in
distress.

But Lear just replied bitterly, "The storm in
my heart is far greater than the storm out here…
I fear I'm losing my mind."

*M*eanwhile, without realising it, Gloucester was giving Edmund another wicked idea...

"Regan and Cornwall have forbidden me even to mention the king's name, but I *must* go after him and see if I can help. If they ask for me, say I'm sick," he told his son. "I can see trouble brewing between Cornwall and Albany. I've also received an important letter which *nobody* must see! It's locked away," he added. "But I can tell you this – the king's suffering will soon be avenged!"

Edmund decided that Cornwall should know about the letter *instantly*.

Eventually, Kent persuaded his king to shelter in a hut on the heath. The jester ran in, but flew out again in a panic.

"There's an evil spirit in there!" he shrieked.

But when Lear and Kent entered the hut they only found a half-naked lunatic, Poor Tom, shivering in the cold. Neither of them saw that it was Edgar in disguise, dancing about, gabbling nonsense.

But King Lear wasn't afraid of him. "This fellow is probably only a father who has given everything he possessed to his daughters," he commented bitterly.

When Gloucester finally caught up with the king the storm was still raging.

"Your daughters don't want me to help you," he explained. "But I *had* to come and take you to safety."

Kent and the jester begged King Lear to let Gloucester help, but he refused unless Poor Tom came too.

"The king's madness is no surprise," thought Gloucester. "His daughters want him dead. I'm nearly crazy myself over the son who's turned against me."

So Gloucester let Poor Tom come with them, not realizing that he was his own son. Neither did he recognize his old friend, Kent.

$\mathcal{A}$t Gloucester's castle, Edmund had stolen the important letter and was showing it to the Duke of Cornwall. "This letter proves that my father and the King of France are plotting against you," Edmund said slyly.

"I'll have my revenge on Gloucester," said Cornwall, furiously. "Edmund, you will be earl in your father's place. Find out where he is!"

Edmund departed immediately. The plan was working just as he had intended.

Gloucester took Lear and his jester, and the disguised Kent and Edgar, to shelter in a nearby farmhouse. He left them to rest and went back to his castle to find out the latest events.

But he returned with shocking news. "The king's enemies are plotting to kill him! There's no time to lose – Caius, you must take King Lear to Dover where I know he'll find friends to protect him."

*A*t Gloucester's castle, Cornwall was issuing orders to his servants.

"Take this letter to the Duke of Albany. Tell him the French army has landed in Dover. And bring that traitor, Gloucester, to me. You, Edmund, escort Goneril to her husband—"

Then Cornwall was interrupted by Oswald with more alarming news. "My Lord of Gloucester has helped the king to escape," he gasped. "Lear's heading for Dover!"

Gloucester was soon captured and dragged back to his castle, where Cornwall ordered him to be bound tightly to a chair.

Gloucester protested but Cornwall demanded, "Where have you sent the king?"

"To Dover," Gloucester replied. "I couldn't stand by and watch his daughters treat him so cruelly…"

"I'll make sure that you never watch anyone or anything again!" shouted Cornwall. And in a frenzied rage he tore out Gloucester's eyes.

One of Gloucester's horrified servants drew his sword and slashed at Cornwall, badly wounding him.

"Where's Edmund?" Gloucester whispered in agony.

"Your son hates you," said Regan spitefully. "It was Edmund who told us you were in league with the King of France."

Gloucester was appalled. "But… if Edmund is against me, then I must have wrongly accused Edgar!"

The blind and bloodied Gloucester allowed himself to be led away from the castle. Soon he was alone on the heath, just like Lear before him.

Still disguised as Poor Tom, Edgar saw the terrible figure staggering towards him. "My poor father!" he whispered to himself. "What on earth can have happened?"

"Do you know the way to Dover, friend?" asked Gloucester, trembling.

Fighting back his emotions, Edgar promised to lead him there.

The two of them had almost reached Dover when they came upon Lear. He was wandering the fields wearing a crown of weeds, talking and singing to himself. "That's the king's voice!" said Gloucester. And the two old men spoke sadly together about the suffering their children had caused them.

Goneril arrived home to be met by Oswald. "The duke supports the French! Be warned, my lady, he is in a fury!" said Oswald. Turning to Edmund, Goneril told him, "Go, before Albany sees you! Return to my sister and help Cornwall to prepare for battle!"

"How can you treat your own father so badly?" raged Albany. "You're a monster!" But Goneril cared nothing for his anger, or for him – anyway, she had begun to prefer Edmund. Then news came of Cornwall's death from his sword wounds. "So, my sister is a widow," Goneril muttered. "Now she may win Edmund!"

Goneril sent Oswald with a message for Edmund. It encouraged him to kill her husband and marry her instead. But the message went astray and it was Edgar who read it. Now he began to see what had been going on...

*A*t the French camp in Dover, Cordelia cared
lovingly for her father. The doctors had dosed
Lear with sleeping medicine and when he first
woke, he did not recognise his youngest
daughter. But at last his mind cleared, and he
knew she was Cordelia. He was filled with
delight – but deeply ashamed of the way he had
treated her.

When the English and French armies met in
battle the French were defeated, and Lear and
Cordelia were taken prisoner at Edmund's
command.

When Albany heard that Edmund had imprisoned Lear and Cordelia, he was furious. Not only this, Goneril and Regan were quarreling over Edmund in front of him. Finally, Albany accused Edmund of behaving like a traitor.

"Where's the proof?" demanded Edmund. "I'll fight whoever accuses me of being a traitor!"

Suddenly, Regan was taken ill and carried away – poisoned, by her sister.

Albany announced that anyone who believed Edmund was a traitor should come forward at the third blast of a trumpet.

On exactly the third blast, Edgar stepped forward, unrecognizable in a suit of armour, and accused his brother.

They fought furiously until Edmund fell, fatally wounded. When he demanded to know his accuser, Edgar pulled off his helmet to show his face.

Goneril now saw that everything was lost. She hurried away and, with a knife, ended her life.

"I arranged for Cordelia to be killed," the dying Edmund whispered, now truly sorry. "Hurry and you might save her."

But it was too late. In came King Lear, carrying the dead body of his beloved daughter. "If only Cordelia could live," he wept. "All my sorrows would vanish. Cordelia! Cordelia!"

"All royal power can now return to Lear, our true king!" pronounced Albany. But his words were wasted. Cordelia's death had finally broken Lear's heart and, collapsing, he died, united at last with the one daughter who had truly loved him.

The Shakespeare Collection

KING LEAR

RETOLD BY ANTHONY MASTERS

Illustrated by Stephen Player

HODDER
Wayland

 *Character list:*

King Lear

Goneril
(Lear's eldest daughter)

Regan
(Lear's second daughter)

Cordelia
(Lear's youngest daughter)

Fool
(Lear's jester)